Dancing Class

by H. M. Ehrlich   pictures by Laura Rader

ORCHARD BOOKS • NEW YORK
An Imprint of Scholastic Inc.

Orchard Books, an imprint of Scholastic Inc.
95 Madison Avenue, New York, NY 10016

Printed in China for Harriet Ziefert, Inc.
The text of this book is set in Soup Bone.
The illustrations are watercolor.

10 9 8 7 6 5 4 3 2 1

Library of Congress Cataloging-in-Publication Data
Ehrlich, H. M.
Dancing class / H. M. Ehrlich ; illustrated by Laura Rader.
p.   cm.
Summary: For Piggy and the other animal dancers, ballet class is an exciting experience.
ISBN 0-531-30300-4 (trade : alk. paper)
[1. Ballet dancing—Fiction. 2. Pigs—Fiction. 3. Animals—Fiction. 4. Stories in rhyme.]
I. Rader, Laura, ill. II. Title.
PZ8.3.Z47 Dan 2001   [E]—dc21   00-23194

For Emma Margolin

—H.M.E.

For H.Z., who has always kept
me on my toes   —L.R.

Piggy runs to
dancing class.

She doesn't want
to be the last.

On go tutus—
slippers, too.

Tights are itchy
when they're new.

Piggy holds on to the bar.

Legs are lifted very far.

Point those feet and *jump* around.

Happier dancers can't be found!

Spinning, twirling, leaping–oh!

Something's wrong with Piggy's toe.

Oops!

Piggy falls and bumps her face.

Teacher says, "It's no disgrace."

Ms. Ashley plays a ballet suite.
Tired dancers rest their feet.

Arms outstretched
up to the sky,

Ballerinas always try.

Smiling dancers in a line . . .

Teacher says, "You're doing fine.

Point those toes . . . touch the sky!

You'll be ballerinas by and by."

Say good-bye, and curtsy now.
All together we take a bow.